Taboo

Taboo
James Branch Cabell

MINT EDITIONS

Taboo was first published in 1921.

This edition published by Mint Editions 2021.

ISBN 9781513295770 | E-ISBN 9781513297279

Published by Mint Editions®

 MINT
EDITIONS

minteditionbooks.com

Publishing Director: Jennifer Newens
Design & Production: Rachel Lopez Metzger
Project Manager: Micaela Clark
Typesetting: Westchester Publishing Services

Laudataque virtus crescit

"*Buttons, a farthing a pair!*
Come, who could buy them of me?
They're round and sound and pretty,
And fit for girls of the city."

Contents

To John S. Sumner   9

Memoir of Sævius Nicanor   11

Prolegomena   13

The Legend   14

    1. How Horvendile Met Fate and Custom   14
    2. How the Garbage Man Came with Forks   14
    3. How Thereupon Ensued a Legal Debate   15
    4. How There Was Babbling in Philistia   16
    5. How It Appeared to the Man in the Street   20

Colophon   22

A Postscript   23

To John S. Sumner

(Agent of the New York Society for the Suppression of Vice)

For no short while my indebtedness to you has been such as to require some sort of public acknowledgment, which may now, I think, be tendered most appropriately by inscribing upon the dedication page of this small volume the name to which you are daily adding in significance.

It is a tribute, however trivial, which serves at least to express my appreciation of your zeal in re-establishing what seemed to the less optimistic a lost cause. I may today confess without much embarrassment that after fifteen years of foiled endeavors my (various) publishers and I had virtually decided that the printing of my books was not likely ever to come under the head of a business venture, but was more properly describable as a rather costly form of dissipation. People here and there would praise, but until you, unsolicited, had volunteered to make me known to the general public, nobody seemed appreciably moved to purchase.

One by one my books had "fallen dead" with disheartening monotony: then—through what motive it would savor of ingratitude to inquire,—you came to remedy all this in the manner of a philanthropic sorcerer, brandishing everywhither your vivifying wand, and the dead lived again. At once, they tell me, the patrons of bookstores began to ask, not only in whispers for the *Jurgen* which you had everywhere so glowingly advertised, but with frank curiosity for "some of the fellow's other books."

Whereon we of course began to "reprint," with, I rejoice to say, results which have been very generally acceptable. Barring a few complaints as to the exiguousness of my writing's salacity,—a salacity which even I confess you amiably exaggerated in attributing to my literary manner all qualities which the average reader most desires in novelists,—there has proved to be in point of fact, as my publishers and I had dubiously believed for years, a gratifying number of persons, living dispersedly about America, prepared to like my books when these books were brought to their attention. The difficulty had been that we did not know how to reach these widely scattered, congenial readers. But you—like Sir James Barrie's hero—"found a way."

I cannot say, in candor, that your method of exegetical criticism has always and in every respect appealed to me. Its applicability, for one thing, seems so universal that it might, for aught I know, be employed to interpret the dicta of Ackermann and Macrobius, or even the canons of Doctors Matthews and Sherman herein cited, and thus open dire vistas wherein critic would prey on critic, and the most respectable would be locked in fratricidal strife. Moreover, I have applied your method to many of the Mother Goose rhymes with rather curious results. . . But happily, I have here to confess to you, not any disputable literary standards I may harbor, but only my unarguable debt.

In brief, your aid obtained for me overnight the hearing I had vainly sought for a long while; and of such thaumaturgy my appreciation will never be, I trust, inadequate. I therefore grasp at the first chance to express this appreciation in—as I have said,—a form which seems not quite inept.

Dumbarton Grange
December, 1920

Of *The Mulberry Grove* the following editions have been collated:

(1) The *editio princeps* of Mansard 1475. An excellent edition, having, says Garnier, "nearly all the authority of an MS." This edition served as the basis of all subsequent editions up to that of Tribebos, 1553, which then took the lead up to the time of Bülg, who judiciously reverted to that of Mansard.
(2) Bülg, in 4 vols. Strasburg. 1786–89. And in 2 vols. Strasburg. 1786. Both editions containing the Dirghic text with a Latin version, and the scholia and indices.
(3) Musgrave, concerning whose edition Garnier is of opinion that, though it appeared later, yet it had been made use of by Bülg. 2 vols. Oxon. 1800. Reprinted, 3 vols. Oxon. 1809–10.
(4) Vanderhoffen, with scholia, notes, and indices. 7 vols. London. 1807–25. His notes reprinted separately. Leipsic. 1824.

Memoir of Sævius Nicanor

Saevius Nicanor Marci libertus negabit

> *"She went to the tailor's*
> *To buy him a coat;*
> *When she came back*
> *He was riding the goat."*

Sævius Nicanor, one of the earliest of the Grammarians, says Suetonius, first acquired fame and reputation by his teaching; and, besides, made commentaries, the greater part of which, however, were said to have been borrowed. He also wrote a satire, in which he informs us that he was a free man, and had a double cognomen.

It is reported that in consequence of some aspersion attached to the character of his writing, he retired into Sardinia, and, says Oriphyles, devoted the remainder of his days to the composition of sardonic[1] literature.

He is quoted by Macrobius, whereas divers references to Nicanor in *La Haulte Histoire de Jurgen* would seem to show that this writer was viewed with considerable esteem in mediæval times. Latterly his work has been virtually unknown.

Robert Burton, for the rest, cites Sævius Nicanor in the 1620 edition of *The Anatomy of Melancholy* (this passage was subsequently remodeled) in terms which have the unintended merit of conveying a very fair notion of the old Grammarian's literary ethics:—

"As a good housewife out of divers fleeces weaves one piece of cloth (saith Sævius Nicanor), I have laboriously collected this Cento out of divers Writers, and that *sine injuria*, I have wronged no authors, but given every man his own; which Sosimenes so much commends in Nicanor, he stole not whole verses, pages, tracts, as some do nowadays, concealing their Authors' names, but still said this was Cleophantus', that Philistion's, that Mnesides', so said Julius Bassus, so Timaristus, thus far Ophelion: I cite and quote mine own Authors (which howsoever some illiterate scribblers account pedantical, as a cloak of ignorance and opposite to their affected

---

1. Ackermann reads "Sardinian." It is not certain whether the adjective employed is (Greek: sardanios) or (Greek: sardanikos). I suspect that Oriphyles here makes an intentional play upon the words.

fine style, I must and will use) *sumpsi, non surripui*, and what Varro *de re rustica* speaks of bees, *minime malificæ quod nullius opus vellicantes faciunt deterius*, I can say of myself no less heartily than Sosimenes his laud of Nicanor."

PROLEGOMENA

Nec caput habentia, nec caudam

*"I had a little husband, no bigger than my thumb,
I put him in my pint-pot, and there I bid him drum."*

P re-eminently the most engaging feature of a topic which pure chance and impure idiocy have of late conspired to pull about in the public prints,—I mean the question of "indecency" in writing,—is the patent ease with which this topic may be disposed of. Since time's beginning, every age has had its literary taboos, selecting certain things—more or less arbitrarily, but usually some natural function—as the things which must not be written about. To violate any such taboo so long as it stays prevalent is to be "indecent": and that seems absolutely all there is to say concerning this topic, apart from furnishing some impressive historical illustration. . .

The most striking instance which my far from exhaustive researches afford, sprang from the fact, perhaps not very generally known, that the natural function of eating, which nowadays may be discussed intrepidly anywhere, was once regarded by the Philistines, of at all events the Shephelah and the deme of Novogath, as being unmentionable. This ancient tenet of theirs, indeed, is with such clearness emphasized in a luckily preserved fragment from the Dirghic, or pre-Ciceronian Latin, of Sævius Nicanor that the readiest way to illustrate the chameleon-like traits of literary indecency appears to be to record, as hereinafter is recorded, what of this legend survives.

Bülg and Vanderhoffen, be it said here, are agreed that it is to this legend Milton has referred in his *Areopagitica*, in a passage sufficiently quaint-seeming to us (for whom a more advanced civilization has secured the right of free speech) to warrant an abridged citation:—

"What advantage is it to be a man, over it is to be a boy at school, if serious and elaborate writings, as if they were no more than the theme of a grammar lad under his pedagogue, must not be uttered without the cursory eyes of a temporizing and extemporizing licenser? whenas all the writer teaches, all he delivers, is but under the tuition, under the correction of his patriarchal licenser, to blot or alter what precisely accords not with the hide-bound humor which he calls his judgment? What is it but a servitude like that imposed by the Philistines?"

The Legend

Fit ex his consuetudo, inde natura

"I love little pussy,
Her fur is so warm."

1. How Horvendile Met Fate and Custom

Now, AT ABOUT THE TIME that the Tyrant Pedagogos fell into disfavor with his people, avers old Nicanor (as the curious may verify by comparing Lib. X, Chap. 28 of his *Mulberry Grove*), passed through Philistia a clerk whom some called Horvendile, travelling by compulsion from he did not know where toward a goal which he could not divine. So this Horvendile said, "I will make a book of this journeying, for it seems to me a rather queer journeying."

They answered him: "Very well, but if you have had dinner or supper by the way, do you make no mention of it in your book. For it is a law among us, for the protection of our youth, that eating[2] must never be spoken of in any of our writing."

Horvendile considered this a curious enactment, but it seemed only one among the innumerable mad customs of Philistia. So he shrugged, and he made the book of his journeying, and of the things which he had seen and heard and loved and hated and had put by in the course of his passage among ageless and unfathomed mysteries.

And in the book there was nowhere any word of eating.

2. How the Garbage Man Came with Forks

Now TO THE BOOK WHICH Horvendile had made comes presently a garbage-man, newly returned from foreign travel for his health's sake, whose name was John. And this scavenger cried, "Oh, horrible! for here is very shameless mention of a sword and a spear and a staff."

"That now is true enough," says Horvendile, "but wherein lies the harm?"

---

2. Such at least is the generally received rendering. Ackermann, following Bülg's probably spurious text, disputes that this is the exact meaning of the noun.

"Why, one has but to write 'a fork' here, in the place of each of these offensive weapons, and the reference to eating is plain."

"That also is true, but it would be your writing and not my writing which would refer to eating."

John said, "Abandoned one, it is the law of Philistia and the holy doctrine of St. Anthony Koprologos that if anybody chooses to understand any written word anywhere as meaning 'to eat,' the word henceforward has that meaning."

"Then you of Philistia have very foolish laws."

To which John the Scavenger sagely replied: "Ah, but if laws exist they ought to fairly and impartially and without favoritism be enforced until amended or repealed. Much of the unsettled condition prevailing in the country at the present time can be traced directly to a lack of law enforcement in many directions during past years."

"Now I misdoubt if I understand you, Messire John, for your infinitives are split beyond comprehension. And when you talk about the non-enforcement of anything in many directions, even though these directions were during past years, I find it so confusing that the one thing of which I can be quite certain is that it was never you whom the law selected to pass upon and to amend all books."

This Horvendile says foolishly, not knowing it is an axiom among the Philistines that literary expression is best controlled by somebody with no misleading tenderness toward it; and that it is this custom, as they proudly aver, which makes the literature of Philistia what it is.

But John the Garbage-man said nothing at all, the while that he changed nouns to "fork" and "dish," and carefully annotated each verb in the book as meaning "to eat." Thereafter he carried off the book along with his garbage, and with—which was the bewildering part of it—self-evident and glowing self-esteem. And all that watched him spoke the Dirghic word of derision, which is "Tee-Hee."

3. How Thereupon Ensued a Legal Debate

Now Horvendile in his bewilderment consulted with a man of law. And the lawman answered a little peevishly, by reason of the fact that age had impaired his digestive organs, and he said, "But of course you are a lewd fellow if you have been suspected of writing about eating."

"Sir," replies Horvendile, "I would have you consider that if your parents and your grandparents had not eaten, your race would have perished, and you would never have been born. I would have you consider that if you and your wife had not eaten, again your race would have perished, and neither of you would ever have lived to have the children for whose protection, as men tell me, you of Philistia avoid all mention of eating."

"Yes, for the object of this most righteous law," declares the lawman, "is to protect those whose character is not so completely formed as to be proof against the effect of meat market reports and grocery advertisements and menu folders and other such provocatives to gluttony."

"—Yet I would have you consider how little is to be gained by attempting to conceal even from the young the inevitability of this natural function, so long as dogs eat publicly in the streets, and the poultry regale themselves just as candidly, and the house-flies also. Instead, the knowledge that this function is not to be talked about induces furtive and misleading discussion among these children, and, though lack of proper instruction in the approved etiquette of eating, they often commit deplorable errors—"

To which the man of law replied, still with a bewildering effect of talking very wisely and patiently: "Ah, but it does not matter at all whether or not the function of eating is practised and is inevitable to the nature and laws of our being. The law merely considers that any mention of eating is apt to inflame an improper and lewd appetite, particularly in the young, who are always ready to eat: and therefore any such mention is an obscene libel."

4. How There Was Babbling in Philistia

Now Horvendile, yet in bewilderment, lamented, and he fled from the man of law. Thereafter, in order to learn what manner of writing was most honored by the Philistines, this Horvendile goes into an academy where the faded old books of Philistia were stored, along with yesterday's other leavings.

And as he perturbedly inspected these old books, one of the fifty mummies which were installed in this Academy of Starch and Fetters, with a hundred lackeys to attend them, spoke vexedly to Horvendile, saying, as it was the custom of these mummies to say, before this could be said to them, "I never heard of you before."

"Ah, sir, it is not that which is troubling me," then answered Horvendile: "but rather, I am troubled because the book of my journeying has been suspected of encroachment upon gastronomy. Now I notice your most sacred volume here begins with a very remarkable myth about the fruit of a tree in the middle of a garden, and goes on to speak of the supper which Lot shared with two angels and with his daughters also, and of the cakes which Tamar served to Amnon, and to speak over and over again of eating—"

"Of course," replies the mummy, yawning, because he had heard this silly sort of talking before.

"I notice that your most honored poet, here where the dust is thickest, from the moment he began by writing about certain painted berries which mocked the appetite of Dame Venus, and about a repast from which luxurious Tarquin retired like a full-fed hound or a gorged hawk, speaks continually of eating. And I notice that everybody, but particularly the young person, is encouraged to read these books, and other ancient books which speak very explicitly indeed of eating—"

"Of course," again replies the mummy (who had been for many years an exponent of dormitive literacy)—"of course, young persons ought to read them: for all these books are classics, and we who were more obviously the heirs of the ages, and the inheritors of European culture, used frequently to discuss these books in Paff's beer-cellar."

"Well, but does the indecency of this word 'eating' evaporate out of it as the years pass, so that the word is hurtful only when very freshly written!"

The mummy blinked so wisely that you would never have guessed that the brains and viscera of all these mummies had been removed when the embalmers, Time and Conformity, were preparing these fifty for the Academy of Starch and Fetters. "Young man, I doubt if the majority of us here in the academy are deeply interested in this question of eating, for reasons unnecessary to specify. But before estimating your literary pretensions, I must ask if you ever frequented Paff's beer-cellar?"

Horvendile said, "No."

Now this mummy was an amiable and cultured old relic, unshakably made sure of his high name for scholarship by the fact that he had written dozens of books which nobody else had even read. So he said, friendlily enough: "Then that would seem to settle your pretensions. To have talked twaddle in Paff's beer-cellar is the one real proof of literary merit, no matter what sort of twaddle you may have written in your book, or in many books, as I am here in this academy to attest. Moreover, I am old enough to remember when cookery-books were sold openly upon the newsstands, and in consequence I am very grateful to the garbage-man, who, in common with all other intelligent persons, has never dreamed of meddling with anything I wrote."

"But, sir," says Horvendile, "do you esteem a scavenger, who does not pretend to specialize in anything save filth, to be the best possible judge of books?"

"He may be an excellent critic if only he indeed belongs to the forthputting Philistine stock: that proviso is most important, though, for, as I recently declared, we have very dangerous standards domiciled in the midst of us, that are only too quickly raised—"

Says Horvendile, with a shudder: "You speak ambiguously. But still, in criticizing books—"

"Plainly, young man, you do not appreciate that the essential qualifications for a critic of Philistine literature are," said this mummy bewilderingly, "to have set off fireworks in July, to have played ball in a vacant lot, and to have repeated what Spartacus said to the gladiators."[3]

"No, no, the essential thing is not quite that," observed an attendant lackey, a really clever writer, who wrote, indeed, far more intelligently than he thought. He was a professor of patriotism, and prior to being embalmed in the academy he had charge of the postgraduate work in atavism and superior sneering. "No, my test is not quite that, and if you venture to disagree with me about this or anything else you are a ruthless Hun and an impudent Jew. No, the garbage-man may very well be an excellent judge: for by my quite infallible test the one thing requisite for a critic of our great Philistine literature is an ability to induce within himself such an internal disturbance as resembles a profound murmur of ancestral voices—"

"But, oh, dear me!" says Horvendile, embarrassed by such talk.

"—And to experience a mysterious inflowing," continued the other, "of national experience—"

"The function is of national experience undoubtedly," said Horvendile, "but still—"

---

3. It is a gratifying tribute to the permanence of æsthetic canons to record that Dr. Brander Matthews (connected with Columbia University) has, in an article upon "Alien Views of American Literature," contributed to the *New York Times* of 14 November, 1920, accepted these three qualifications as the essential groundwork for a literary critic even today; although Dr. Matthews is inclined, as a concession to modernism, to add to the list an ability to recite Webster's Reply to Hayne. Since Dr. Matthews frankly states that he has been incited to this recital of a critic's needs by (in his happy wording) "the alien angle" of "standards domiciled in the midst of us," it is sincerely to be hoped that his requirements may be met forthwith.

"—Whenever he meditates," concluded this lackey bewilderingly, "upon the name of Bradford and six other surnames.[4] At all events, I have turned wearily from your book, you bolshevistic German Jew—"

"But I," says Horvendile feebly, "am not a German Jew."

"Oh, yes, you are, and so is everybody else whose literary likings are not my likings. I repeat, then, that I have turned wearily from your book. Whether or not it treats of eating, its implication is clearly that the Philistia which has developed Bradford and six other appellations perfectly adapted to produce murmurings and inflowings in properly constituted persons,—and which Philistia, as I have elsewhere asserted, is today as always a revolting country whenever it condemns,—has had no civilised cultural atmosphere worth mentioning. So your book fails to connect itself vitally with our great tradition as to our literature, and I find nowhere in your book any ascending sun heralded by the lookouts."

"No more do I," said Horvendile; "but I would have imagined you were more interested in lunar phenomena, and even so—"

"Moreover," now declared another mummy (this was a Moor, called P.E.M., or the Peach,[5] who through some oversight had not been embalmed, but only pickled in vinegar, to the detriment of his disposition),—"moreover, I am not at all in sympathy with any protest whatever against the scavenger, for it might be taken as an excuse for what they are pleased to call art."

All groaned at this abominable word. And then another lackey cried, "You are a prosperous and affected pseudo-littérateur!" and all the mummies spoke sepulchrally the word of derision, which is "Tee-Hee":

---

4. Sævius Nicanor does not record the wonder-working surnames employed to produce this ancient, ante-Aristotlean (Greek: *katharsis*), and they are not certainly known. But, quite unaided, I believe, by old Nicanor's hint, Dr. Stuart Pratt Sherman (the accomplished editor of divers contributions to literature, and the author of several books) has discovered, through a series of interesting experiments in vivisection, that the one needful endowment for a critic of American letters is the power to induce within himself "a profound murmur of ancestral voices, and to experience a mysterious inflowing of national experience, in meditating on the names of Mark Twain, Whitman, Thoreau, Lincoln, Emerson, Franklin, and Bradford." Compare "Is There Anything To Be Said for Literary Tradition," in *The Bookman* for October, 1920. Any candid consideration of Dr. Sherman's phraseology, here as elsewhere, cannot fail to suggest that he has happily re-discovered the long-lost critical abracadabra of Philistia.

5. Codman annotates this: "Synonyms, since P.E.M. is obviously *Persicum Esculentum Malum*—that is, the peach; 'which,' says Macrobius, 'although it rather belongs to the tribe of apples, Sævius reckons as a species of nut.'"

and many said also, "The scavenger has never meddled with us, and we never heard of you," and there was much other incoherent foolishness.

But Horvendile had fled, bewildered by the ways of Philistia's adepts in starch and fetters, and bewildered in particular to note that a mummy, so generally esteemed a kindly and well-meaning fossil, appeared quite honestly to believe that all literature came out of the beer-cellar of Paff, or Pfaff, or had some similarly Teutonic sponsor; and that handball was the best training for literary criticism; and that the cookery-books of fifty years ago had something to do with Horvendile's account of his journeying, from he did not know where toward a goal which he could not divine, now being in the garbage pile. It troubled Horvendile because so many persons seemed to regard the old fellow half seriously.

5. How It Appeared to the Man in the Street

STILL, HORVENDILE WAS NOT QUITE routed by these heaped follies. "For, after all," says Horvendile, in his own folly, "it is for the normal human being that books are made, and not for mummies and men of law and scavengers."

So Horvendile went through a many streets that were thronged with persons travelling by compulsion from they did not know where toward a goal which they could not divine, and were not especially bothering about. And it was evening, and to this side and to that side the men and women of Philistia were dining. Everywhere maids were passing hot dishes, and forks were being thrust into these dishes, and each was eating according to his ability and condition. No matter how poverty-stricken the household, the housewife was serving her poor best to the goodman. For with luncheon so long past, all the really virile men of Philistia were famished, and stood ready to eat the moment, they had a dish uncovered.

So it befell that Horvendile encountered a representative citizen, who was coming out of a representative restaurant with a representative wife.

And the sight of this representative citizen was to Horvendile a tonic joy and a warming of the heart. For this man, and each of the thousands like him, as Horvendile reflected, had been within this hour sedately dining with his wife,—neither of them eating with the zest and vigor of their first youth, perhaps, but sharing amicably the more moderate refreshment which middle-age requires,—without being at any particular pains to conceal the fact from anybody. Here was then, after all, the strong and sure salvation of Philistia, in this quiet, unassuming common-sense, which dealt with the facts of life as facts, the while that the foolish laws, and the academical and stercoricolous nonsense of Philistia, reverberated as remotely and as unheeded as harmless summer thunder.

"Sir," says elated Horvendile, "I perceive that you two have just been eating, and that emboldens me to ask you—"

But at this point Horvendile found he had been knocked down, because the parents of the representative citizen had taught him from his earliest youth that any mention of eating was highly indecent in the presence of gentlewomen. And for Horvendile, recumbent upon the pavement, it was bewildering to note the glow of honest indignation in the face of the representative citizen, who waited there, in front of the restaurant he usually patronized. . .

Colophon

Here, rather vexatiously, the old manuscript breaks off. But what survives and has been cited of this fragment amply shows you, I think, that even in remote Philistia, whenever this question of "indecency" arose, everybody (including the accused) was apt to act very foolishly. It has attested too, I hope, the readiness with which you may read ambiguities into the most respectable of authors; as well as the readiness with which a fanatical training may lead you to imagine some underlying impropriety in all writing about any natural function, even though it be a function so time-hallowed and general as that to which this curious Dirghic legend refers.

A Postscript

(French of C.J.P. Garnier)

The swine that died in Gadara two thousand years ago
Went mad in lofty places, with results that all men know—
Went mad in lofty places through long rooting in the dirt,
Which (even for swine) begets at last soul-satisfying hurt.
The swine in lofty places now are matter for no song
By any prudent singer, but—*how long, O Lord, how long?*

A Note About the Author

James Branch Cabell (1879–1958) was an American writer of escapist and fantasy fiction. Born into a wealthy family in the state of Virginia, Cabell attended the College of William and Mary, where he graduated in 1898 following a brief personal scandal. His first stories began to be published, launching a productive decade in which Cabell's worked appeared in both *Harper's Monthly Magazine* and *The Saturday Evening Post*. Over the next forty years, Cabell would go on to publish fifty-two books, many of them novels and short-story collections. A friend, colleague, and inspiration to such writers as Ellen Glasgow, H.L. Mencken, Sinclair Lewis, and Theodore Dreiser, James Branch Cabell is remembered as an iconoclastic pioneer of fantasy literature.

A Note from the Publisher

Spanning many genres, from non-fiction essays to literature classics to children's books and lyric poetry, Mint Edition books showcase the master works of our time in a modern new package. The text is freshly typeset, is clean and easy to read, and features a new note about the author in each volume. Many books also include exclusive new introductory material. Every book boasts a striking new cover, which makes it as appropriate for collecting as it is for gift giving. Mint Edition books are only printed when a reader orders them, so natural resources are not wasted. We're proud that our books are never manufactured in excess and exist only in the exact quantity they need to be read and enjoyed.

Discover more of your favorite classics with Bookfinity™.

- Track your reading with custom book lists.
- Get great book recommendations for your personalized Reader Type.
- Add reviews for your favorite books.
- AND MUCH MORE!

Visit **bookfinity.com** and take the fun Reader Type quiz to get started.

Enjoy our classic and modern companion pairings!